For Stephen and Liz Baird,
with many thanks – SG

For Paulina, Mary Elizabeth,
Dorothy and Valentina McNeill – ET

Published by Bloomsbury, New York and London
Distributed to the trade by St. Martin's Press
Printed in Belgium by Proost

Library of Congress Cataloging-in-Publication Data
Grindley, Sally.
No trouble at all / by Sally Grindley ; illustrated by Eleanor Taylor.—1ˢᵗ U.S. ed.
p. cm. Summary Grandfather Bear thinks his cubs are so wonderful,
he cannot imagine them being naughty.
ISBN 1-58234-757-3
(alk. paper) [1. Grandfather—Fiction. 2. Sleepovers—Fiction. 3. Behavior—Fiction. 4.
Bears—Fiction.] I. Taylor, Elarnor, 1969-, ill. II. Title.
PZ7.G88446 No 2002 [E]—dc21   2001043982

First U.S. Edition 2002

1 3 5 7 9 10 8 6 4 2

Bloomsbury USA Children's Books
175 Fifth Avenue
New York, NY 10010

No Trouble at All

by Sally Grindley
illustrated by Eleanor Taylor

BLOOMSBURY
CHILDREN'S
BOOKS

Shhh! They're fast asleep.
Don't wake them up.

They're such good little
bears when they come
to stay.

I just have to say it's time
for bed, and off they go,
as good as gold.

When I was their age
I was full of mischief.

These old houses are full of strange noises.
I'd better just check those little bears
aren't frightened.

Not a sound.
I must have worn
them out.

I'll just fetch
my slippers.

Ah, here they are.

Their mother says those little bears can be very naughty. I'm sure that can't be true.

What was that?

I guess I didn't close the door properly. Silly of me.

It's a beautiful night.
If it's sunny tomorrow
we'll all go for a picnic.

I'll just fetch
the picnic basket
from the shed.

Here we are. Tomorrow
I'll fill it with sandwiches
and cakes and chocolates and
drinks and off we'll go.

They deserve a treat, those
little bears. They're absolutely
no trouble.

No trouble at all.

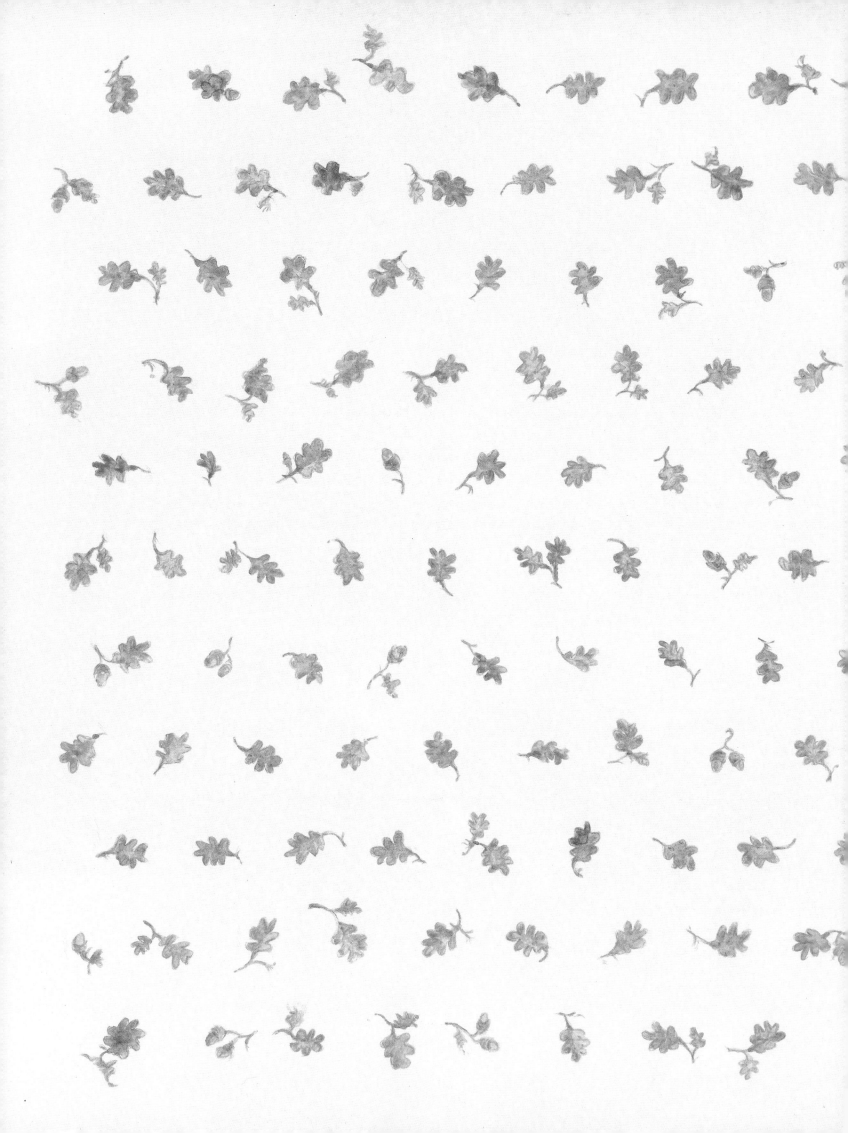